YOUR BEST SELF

I Can Be Respectful

written by Meredith Rusu

illustrated by Alexandra Colombo

Children's Press®
An imprint of Scholastic Inc.

Special thanks to Dr. Ann (Nancy) Close, assistant professor of the Yale School of Medicine and member of the Child Study Center at Yale University, for her insight into the development of children in early childhood.

Library of Congress Cataloging-in-Publication Data available
ISBN 978-1-5461-0154-3 (library binding) | ISBN 978-1-5461-0155-0 (paperback)

10 9 8 7 6 5 4 3 2 1 25 26 27 28 29

Printed in China 62
First edition, 2025

Book design by Kathleen Petelinsek

TABLE OF CONTENTS

I Can Be Respectful

Hi! My name is Eliza. And it is **Respect** Week at my school.

Respect means treating people the way you want to be treated. My teacher says when we give respect, we get respect back.

She asked us to fill out our "Respect Charts" this week. Here we go!

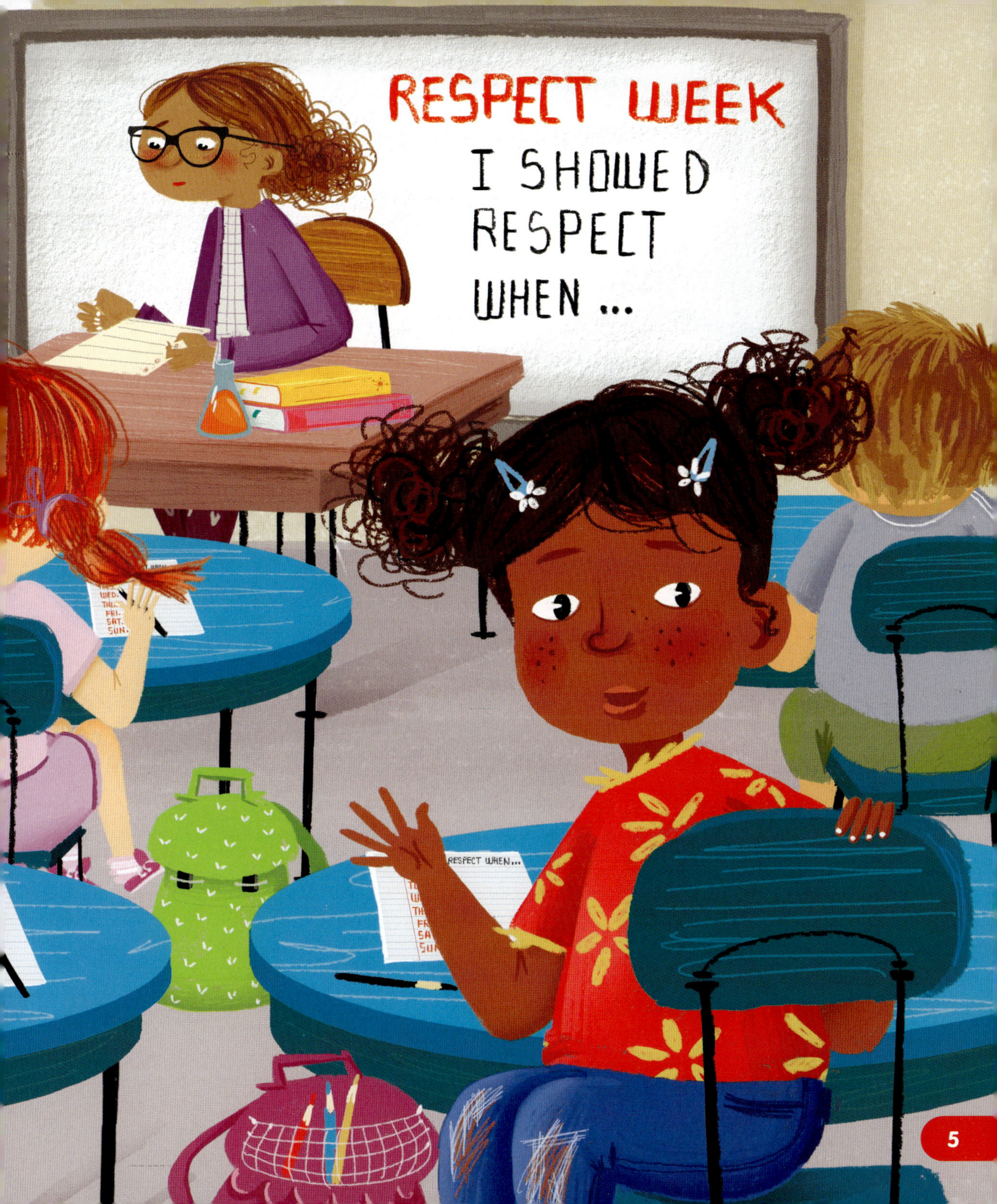
RESPECT WEEK
I SHOWED RESPECT WHEN ...
RESPECT WHEN...

MONDAY

I can be respectful by using **polite** words.
I kindly say "please" when I want something.
And "thank you" when I get it.

TUESDAY

I can be respectful by not complaining.
The librarian doesn't read the story I wanted.
That makes me feel **frustrated**.
But I show respect by not yelling
and making a fuss.

The Boy
Who Cried
Wolf
JACK
AND THE
BEAN
STALK

I can be respectful by listening to my friend. She tells me, "Please don't color on my picture!" I had a really good idea to add a rainbow. But it's her drawing, not mine.

GIVE RESPECT, GET RESPECT

My friend asks to see my rainbow on another piece of paper.

I can be respectful by paying **attention**.
A farmer is visiting our class today.
The baby chicks are so cute,
I want to say "Ooh!" and "Ahh!"
But I sit quietly and listen instead.

GIVE RESPECT, GET RESPECT

I get a turn to hold the chicks, and then I can say "Ooh!" and "Ahh!"

I SHOWED RESPECT WHEN...
MON. I SAID PLEASE AND THANK YOU
TUES. I DID NOT GET MAD
WED. I LISTENED
THURS.

FRIDAY

I can be respectful by not **arguing**.
Suzy says she doesn't like the color purple.
I think purple is the best color ever!
But we don't have to all like the same things.
It is okay to **disagree**.

GIVE RESPECT, GET RESPECT

Suzy gives me the purple hoop because she knows it's my favorite.

SATURDAY

I can be respectful by holding the door for someone. I was here first. And I'm excited to go inside. But helping someone shows I care.

GIVE RESPECT, GET RESPECT

The lady says I'm very **thoughtful**.

SED
TOY SHOP
$10
$5
$3
$7

Stories

I can be respectful by forgiving my sister. She accidentally spilled juice on my shirt. Seeing the stains makes me want to scream! But I don't. It was just an accident.

GIVE RESPECT, GET RESPECT

My sister helps clean my shirt.

I can be respectful by saying,
"I'm sorry" to my parents.
I was worried we'd be late for school.
So I stamped my foot and yelled, "Hurry up!"
But I should have been more patient.

GIVE RESPECT, GET RESPECT

My parents say they will try to hurry.

CELEBRATE RESPECT!

I can be respectful by raising my hand quietly to share my chart. Everyone wants to go first. But shouting out is **rude**.

GIVE RESPECT, GET RESPECT

The teacher says because I was respectful, I can present first! And we even get medals for filling out our charts.

Our teacher is so proud of us! She says we built a respectful classroom **community** this week. She says she is sure it will last all year. I love being respectful! It makes me feel happy . . . and safe!

CELEBRATE
RESPECT!

WHAT IS RESPECT?

Have you ever heard a grown-up say, "Show some respect!"? They may have been talking about how you spoke to a grandparent or even how you played with your toys.

So what is respect? As you have seen, respect means treating others the way you would want to be treated. When you use kind words, that's respect. When you appreciate someone for who they are, that's respect. Showing respect builds trust. And it makes people feel safe.

Read the sentences on the next page with a grown-up. How would each make you feel? Which ones do you think show respect?

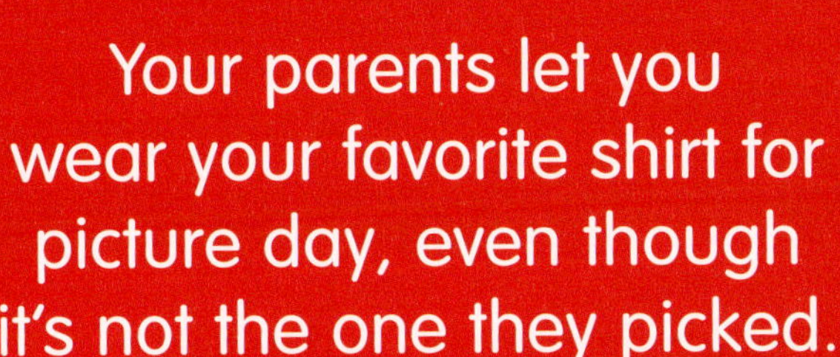

1

Your parents let you wear your favorite shirt for picture day, even though it's not the one they picked.

2

You wait until your teacher is done speaking to ask a question.

3

A kid steps on your backpack and doesn't say "sorry."

4

Your cousin unwraps your birthday present without asking.

5

Your friend says, "May I please play with your basketball?"

ANSWERS: Numbers 1, 2, and 5 show respect.

GIVE RESPECT, GET RESPECT!

Try having each member of your family make a Respect Chart. Each day, write down one way you showed respect to someone else. At the end of the week, have everyone read their charts out loud. Then make one another Respect Medals to proudly wear!

Use the chart on the next page as an example to get you started.

I SHOWED RESPECT WHEN...

MONDAY

I put away my toys the first time I was asked to do it.

TUESDAY

I said, "May I be excused?" after I finished eating dinner.

WEDNESDAY

THURSDAY

FRIDAY

GLOSSARY

arguing (AHR-gyoo-ing) to disagree while talking about or discussing something

The kids kept arguing about who was first in line.

attention (uh-TEN-shuhn) If you pay attention, you concentrate on one thing.

I paid attention while the teacher explained the math problem.

community (kuh-MYOO-ni-tee) a place and the people who are in it

The students were all part of the classroom community.

disagree (dis-uh-GREE) to have a different opinion

I disagree with my mom's rule that video games aren't allowed on school days.

frustrated (FRUHS-tray-tid) feeling helpless or discouraged

I felt frustrated that the pool was closed because of rain.

polite (puh-LITE) having good manners; being well behaved and respectful to others

Mary Alice was always polite when asking for a treat.

respect (ri-SPEKT) thinking highly of someone and accepting somebody for who they are, even when they're different from you or you don't agree with them

The baseball team treated their opponents with respect.

rude (rood) bad-mannered or offensive, as in rude behavior or a rude answer

The little boy was so rude, he stuck his tongue out at the grown-up.

thoughtful (THAWT-fuhl) considering the needs and wants of others

It was thoughtful of Johnny to hold the door for the old lady.

ABOUT THE AUTHOR

Meredith Rusu has written more than 100 children's books. She lives in New Jersey with her husband and two young sons whom she tries (very hard!) to inspire to be respectful every day.

ABOUT THE ILLUSTRATOR

Alexandra Colombo has illustrated more than 100 books that have been published all over the world. She loves walking in the woods, writing poetry, and discovering new places. She lives in Italy with her turtle, Carlo, and her dog, Ary.